ant and ant

and the
Cave Dwellers

anthony ant
and the
Cave Dwellers

STORY BY JOHN GRANT

Based on the TV series

INSPIRED BY THE BOOKS OF LORNA AND GRAHAM PHILPOT

A Dolphin ★ Paperback

First published in Great Britain in 1999
as a Dolphin Paperback
by Orion Children's Books
a division of the Orion Publishing Group Ltd
Orion House
5 Upper St Martin's Lane
London WC2H 9EA

TV series copyright © HIT Entertainment Plc and YTV co-productions 1999
Based on the books by Lorna and Graham Philpot
Illustrations by The County Studio
Illustrations copyright © Orion Children's Books 1999

The right of John Grant to be identified as the author of this work
has been asserted.

A catalogue record for this book is available from the British Library.
Printed in Great Britain

one

It was a beautiful spring day.

"Let's go somewhere," said Anthony, who was hanging around with Billy.

"Yeah, let's do something exciting," said Billy.

"You could help spring-clean my office, if you haven't got anything better to do," said Arnold, Anthony's father. "It's a mess. I can never find anything. Even my spectacles."

"Oh, O.K.," said Anthony. He would

have preferred to be out with the gang, but by spring-cleaning his father's office he might find some really interesting things that could come in useful. "Come on, Billy. See what you can find."

Arnold's office in the museum was a terrible clutter. There was a desk and a chair in the only clear space between filing cabinets, bookcases and stacks of boxes. Books and papers spilled out on to the floor from the shelves around the walls. Anthony loved it. You never knew what weird and wonderful things were hidden away there!

It was a normal spring-clean day in the museum office. Anthony stood on the chair to reach up and put things back on shelves. Arnold moved things about, opening drawers and closing cupboards. He found his spectacles and lost them

again. Several times.

Billy was burrowing about in a dusty corner full of old boxes tied up with string. One of them had burst open and all kinds of bits and pieces had spilled out. Anthony joined Billy on the floor to examine them. In a museum, what looked like rubbish might turn out to be treasure.

Billy picked up a small, shiny object. At least, it was shiny once he had rubbed off the dust. He showed it to Arnold.

"That's a mirror," said Arnold. "Or, rather, it's a piece broken off a Bigfoot mirror. Throw it in the waste bin."

"Can I keep it?" asked Billy.

"If you like," said Arnold.

"Thanks," said Billy. "Hey, Anthony, what have you found?"

Anthony held up a small piece of flat grey stone. There was a pattern scratched on the stone, and a hole near the edge.

"I think I found that on an expedition when I was a very young ant," said Arnold. "I can't remember exactly. I went on several trips."

"Where to?" asked Anthony.

"Into the unknown," said his father. "I can't remember where I picked up the stone. Ask Grandpa Angus. He was there too. He'll know."

Anthony and Billy took the stone to Grandpa Angus. "Rotten memory your father has," grunted Grandpa Angus. "I'm a lot older than he is, and I can remember where we found it. In the Wildlands."

"The Wildlands!" said Anthony. "Where are they?"

"Not so far from here, but it's a hard journey, and it's dangerous. It's bare and bleak and there are wild beasts. There are even supposed to be some ants too. Ne-ant-erthals, they're called. They're

cave dwellers. No one's ever seen one."

"So what's that stone?" asked Anthony.

"Don't know. Young Arnold was always filling his pockets with rubbish," said Grandpa Angus.

"I wonder if Alexi would know," said Anthony. "Come on, Billy, let's go and find her."

Alexi was in a corner of the library, making notes on life in Antville in the olden days. Anthony went up to her and showed her the stone.

"That's nice," said Alexi. "If you put a string through the hole you could wear it round your neck."

"But what do you think it is?" asked Anthony, puzzled.

Alexi took a closer look. She examined the pattern through a magnifying glass. "It reminds me of something," she said.

"I know! I once saw a picture of some patterns made by Ne-ant-erthals thousands of years ago. Maybe Ne-ant-erthals left this stone behind."

"Or maybe they're still there," said Anthony. "Grandpa Angus said there are some in the Wildlands, but no one has ever seen them. I bet I'd see some if I went to the Wildlands."

"Me too!" cried Billy.

"I'd love to see cave ants," said Alexi. "I'd like to live in a cave myself. Just for a while."

"Hey, let's go and find some!" said Anthony. "We can go to the Wildlands ourselves. My father was an explorer ant. So am I. We'll go – us three, and Ruby and Kevin and Terry."

The rest of the gang were keen to see the cave ants. Ruby thought everyone ought to live in caves. Terry thought the cave ants would be incredibly tough. Kevin thought it would be really cool to go to the Wildlands.

They left early next day. Before long Antville was far behind. Now the gang were in strange country. It grew stranger the farther they travelled.

Suddenly, Ruby said, "Listen! Footsteps! Coming this way. Quite a crowd by the sound of them."

The gang waited. Was it the local ants coming to warn off a bunch of trespassers? Or a regiment of soldier ants on the march? But it was neither. Into view around a large pebble came . . . a millipede!

The millipede scowled at the gang.

"Good morning," said Anthony.

"What's good about it?" snapped the millipede.

"I was just going to ask . . ." began Anthony.

"Don't bother," said the millipede. "I'm not in the mood to answer questions. Especially from emmets!"

"Hey!" said Kevin. "Calm down, there's no need to get sore."

"Sore? Sore? Don't speak to me about sore!" snapped the millipede. "I've come a long way. I've a long way to go, and my feet are killing me! All of them! Sore, indeed!" And with that he hurried on his way, muttering, "Emmets! No consideration for others . . .!"

"What's an emmet?" asked Billy.

"It's a very old word," said Alexi. "It means ant!"

"I was just going to ask him if we were going the right way for the Wildlands," said Anthony. "Perhaps this daddy-long-legs can help."

The daddy-long-legs looked down as Anthony looked up to him and shouted, "Could you help us, please?"

"You lost?" said the daddy-long-legs. "You're a long way from home."

"Are we on the right road for the Wildlands?" said Anthony.

"Wildlands?" said the daddy-long-legs. "Hm, you wouldn't catch me wanting to go to the Wildlands. You want to go to the Wildlands? You go! Straight on. You won't like it. It's full of wild animals. Fierce ones!" The long-legged insect spread its wings and drifted off, muttering, "Wildlands! Whatever next?"

"Cheery lot, the people around here," said Terry. "I hope they're more friendly in the Wildlands."

"Well, hello there, kids!" came a lazy-sounding voice. A green grasshopper lay back against a pad of soft moss. "You don't happen to have any fiddle strings on you?" he asked.

"Why?" asked Kevin. "Are you a fiddler?"

"All grasshoppers are fiddlers. Just like all ants are workers," drawled the grasshopper. "It's an old story. The ants work while the grasshopper fiddles."

"Wow," said Kevin. "Some people have all the luck."

"My old dad overdid it," sighed the grasshopper. "Fiddled right through the summer and the autumn into the winter . . . and got himself frozen solid. How's that for luck?"

"I'm sorry we've got no fiddle strings," said Anthony. "We're on our way to the Wildlands."

"Whatever turns you on," said the grasshopper. And he leaned back on the moss and appeared to fall asleep.

two

The gang trudged through a long, narrow valley. When they reached the far end they knew they were in the Wildlands. The land was bare and bleak.

Alexi took a book from her pocket. It was called A Guide to the Wildlands – Survival for Travelling Ants. She opened it and started to read. "The land is bare and bleak. Most of the time the weather is cold."

"Sounds fun," said Kevin. "Why do

the cave ants live in a place like this?"

"Good question," said Alexi. "I'll ask the first Ne-ant-erthal I meet. I'll be on the lookout for one."

She turned back to the book. "Travellers must be on the lookout for the many dangerous creatures which make their home in the Wildlands."

From now on the gang kept a careful watch. Terry brought up the rear, but something was bothering him. He turned and looked back but saw nothing. He waited until the gang were far ahead, then lay down and put his ear to the ground. He listened for a moment. Suddenly he leapt to his feet and ran to catch them up.

"We're being followed," he panted.

"Who by?" asked Anthony.

"I don't know, but I'm sure there's a lot of them and they're coming towards us!" said Terry.

"We'd better take cover," said Anthony.

The gang crouched in the crevices among a pile of pebbles, held their breath, and waited. Soon they could hear the tramp and shuffle of what sounded like an army of feet.

"Another bad-tempered millipede, do you think?" suggested Ruby in a whisper.

But it was a long, hairy creature with many legs. It stopped and sniffed at the ground. Then it reared up the front half of its body. The gang watched a pair of eyes sweeping back and forth. The sight of its open mouth and enormous fangs was terrifying.

Alexi flipped through her book. "A sabre-toothed centipede," she gulped. "The book says it's very dangerous."

"Who needs a book to tell them that?" said Ruby. "That is no puss-moth!"

They stayed very quiet, but the sabre-toothed centipede showed no sign of going. It lowered its body back to the ground again. It was hungry, but it could wait. It could sense ant. Fresh ant!

Terry kept his eye on the monster as he tried to move into a more comfortable position. Ant-size crevices were a tight squeeze for a burly young termite. He stretched one leg and then another, dislodging a small pebble. It rolled to the ground. The sabre-toothed centipede turned its head, but it saw nothing. It settled back to wait.

Terry waited too. Then, gently but steadily, he began to push the pebbles behind him. One moved. And another. A little at a time he began to work his way to the back of the pebble pile.

"What are you doing?" whispered Anthony.

"I'm going to give our furry friend something to take its mind off ants," whispered Terry. He pushed his legs free of the pebbles. One last wriggle and he was out, hidden from the sabre-toothed centipede by the pile of pebbles. Now, if he could take its mind off the ants for long enough, they could escape. He had no real plan. Somehow he had to find a way to distract it.

From their hiding place the gang could see nothing of Terry, and neither could the centipede.

Terry made it to a spot on the ground where the centipede stood between him and the gang. The centipede was growing suspicious. There was a strange scent in the air. Ants it knew, but this was different, and different could mean dangerous. It could smell termite. And there were no termites in the Wildlands.

Except Terry!

Terry looked around for something to use as a weapon. There was a clump of scrubby bushes nearby, and fragments of bark and pieces of twig lay scattered on the ground. It gave him an idea. It was dangerous, but it might just work. He chose a stout piece of twig that seemed to be about the right length. Holding the twig in one hand, he collected handfuls of stones with the others. He jumped out into the open behind the centipede and hurled a shower of stones.

The centipede whirled round. It saw a strange creature facing it. It would make a tasty snack. It rushed upon Terry with all the speed of its many legs, jaws open, and at that moment Terry sprang forward and with all his termite strength wedged the twig into the gaping jaws.

While the angry centipede tried to dislodge the twig, Terry ran back to the gang. "Quick!" he shouted, "before it gets its jaws free!"

The gang scrambled from among the pebbles and ran. When the sabre-toothed centipede was left far behind and they stopped to rest, Terry told them what he had done.

"I hope he gets the twig out of his mouth," said Ruby. "I wouldn't like him to starve. But I didn't fancy becoming his supper!"

three

"**W**hen do we meet a cave ant?" asked Billy.

"Perhaps there aren't any," said Kevin. "Maybe they don't live here anymore. I can't say I blame them."

"Look in your book, Alexi," said Anthony. "How much more wildlife must we be on the lookout for?"

Alexi turned a few pages. "You can take your choice," she said, "of cave ant-lion, the giant elk-beetle . . ."

"What's that?" asked Ruby.

"Same as a stag beetle, but hairy and ten times bigger," said Alexi. "And, of course, the woolly rhinoceros beetle."

"Like the one watching us?" asked Billy nervously.

"Yikes!" exclaimed Kevin. "Where did that come from?"

"It's coming this way!" cried Ruby.

"It's all right," said Terry, "we're down wind of it."

"I don't think," said Anthony, "that makes a lot of difference if it accidentally treads on you. Keep still."

The beetle was in no hurry. It ambled along, head down. Occasionally it stopped and sniffed and looked around before carrying on.

"Look just over there!" hissed Ruby, pointing.

On a slight rise were two more woolly rhinoceros beetles. The gang held their breath as their beetle stopped, turned then trotted off to join the others.

"I think the poor thing was lost," said Ruby.

"In my opinion," said Kevin, "we are too. Where do we go now? I wish we could find a cave ant to ask for directions."

"Hey, take a look at this!" said Alexi suddenly, pointing to a line of footprints. "Those are ant prints. I wonder if it's a cave ant's trail."

"Let's follow it and see where it takes us," said Anthony.

The gang followed the trail as it wound between some big boulders. And there, crouched behind a rock, was an ant, strangely dressed in a scrap of fur.

"It must be a cave ant!" whispered Alexi.

"A real cave ant! Come on, gang!" shouted Kevin, rushing forward.

The cave ant must have heard. He looked round and shouted, "Get down! Here it comes again!"

There was a drone of wings and a rush of wind. A shadow swept over the gang as they threw themselves flat on the ground. Anthony looked up and the stranger signalled him to stay down. There was another rush of wind as the attacker buzzed overhead again and zoomed away into the distance.

"Wow, that was the biggest wasp I've

ever seen!" said Kevin. "We could have been stung. Or eaten."

"You saved our lives!" cried Ruby.

"That's all right," said the stranger. "You ought to have your spears with you, though." And he held up a long, sharp thorn.

"Well, we've found a cave ant," said

Alexi. "You are a cave ant, aren't you?"

"What else? My name's Emmet. What kind of ants are you, anyway? Oh-oh! Heads down!"

The wasp was trying to attack again. Anthony looked round. "Where's Billy?" he cried.

"There he is! Come down, Billy!" shouted Terry.

Billy was on top of the highest boulder. The wasp dived fast out of the sun.

"I can't look!" cried Ruby.

The huge insect was almost on top of Billy when it suddenly veered off. It circled around for another attempt on the little bedbug, and again turned sharply away at the very last moment. As they watched, it did it again. And again. And again! It was no longer flying straight. It collided with the top of a boulder, buzzed for a moment, and flew unsteadily away.

"Billy!" cried Anthony. "What happened? How did you . . . ?"

Billy turned, and a bright flash of light dazzled them for a moment. "My mirror," he laughed. "Grandpa Angus showed me how to tease people by shining the sun in their faces. I just teased that big wasp . . . and it flew away."

"No sense of humour, some wasps," said Kevin.

"I'm glad I met you," said Emmet. "You must come and meet my family. My father is Cave Leader."

Emmet's family cave was very large. And so was his family. His father, the Cave Leader, was a very dignified old ant dressed in soft black and yellow bumble-bee fur. He bent down and shook Billy by the hand.

"You saved my son's life," he said. "You are very brave for one so small. Welcome, young bedbug. You are the first bedbug to visit us."

"I'm not surprised," whispered Kevin to Anthony. "There don't appear to be any beds."

"Nor much else," said Anthony, "except ants."

The whole family came crowding around to meet the strangers. Alexi tried to keep count, but soon gave up. Emmet had parents, grandparents, and dozens of brothers, sisters, aunts, uncles, and cousins, all packed into one family cave.

The Cave Leader clapped some of his hands and announced, "Take your places for supper, everyone."

Two young cave ants came forward and handed each of the gang a large piece of fur. All the others seemed to have one of their own. Then Emmet led them to their places beside his father.

"Hey," said Kevin to Anthony, "where do we sit?"

"No table. No chairs," said Billy.

"What do you expect?" hissed Alexi. "These are cave dwellers. They don't have any tables and chairs."

The old cave ant waved each of the gang to a rock. Now they knew what the pieces of fur were for. The rocks were hard. The fur made them a little less uncomfortable to sit upon.

The cave ants ate and drank from rough clay mugs and plates. They didn't seem to do any cooking – all the food was cold.

Dusk was falling and it was getting darker and darker inside the cave. The gang were hungry, but it was hard to see what they were eating and they had to grope around for it. "Lucky I know where my mouth is," muttered Kevin.

By the time supper was over there was only a glimmer of starlight through the cave entrance, and the gang blundered and tripped over each other as they rose from the meal.

"Bedtime," said Emmet's father, disappearing into the back of the cave. "We've put out some fur rugs for you. Sleep well. Pleasant dreams!"

"I'm ready for bed," said Kevin. "It's been a busy day."

"Where are those rugs?" said Ruby through chattering teeth. "I'm frozen. A bowl of hot soup would have been a good idea."

"Why don't they switch the lights on?" asked Billy.

"They don't have any electricity, silly," said Alexi. "I keep telling you, these are cave ants."

Anthony found the pile of fur rugs. "O.K.," he said, "get bundled up. You'll soon be warm, Ruby."

"These rugs are damp," muttered Terry

as he rolled himself in the extra large one thoughtfully provided for him by their hosts.

But, as Kevin said, it had been a busy day. Soon, apart from the occasional snore, silence descended on the cave. Huddled together for warmth, Anthony, Billy, Ruby, Terry, Alexi and Kevin fell asleep, one by one.

Anthony woke to the sound of voices and footsteps. He sat up and caught a glimpse of figures moving against the moonlight in the cave entrance. He nudged Kevin. "There's something happening," he said.

Kevin sat up. "Eh? What?" he said, half asleep.

A voice spoke from the darkness. "So sorry to disturb you. We're just changing over."

By now, all the gang were awake.

"What does he mean, changing over?" asked Terry.

"Search me," said Kevin.

The gang settled down again, but every time they dropped off, ants watching at the entrance changed places with some other ants. Suddenly the gang woke with a start. The cave echoed to loud shouts. From outside came the sound of roaring and snarling.

The gang leapt to their feet as Emmet called, "Grab some stones. By the entrance!"

There was just enough moonlight to see the cave ants grabbing handfuls of stones that lay on the floor and throwing them hard at something outside in the night. Anthony could just about see something very big and, by the sound of it, something very fierce.

"Cave ant-lion!" shouted Emmet. "Worse than cave woolly bear. Take that!" He hurled a large stone at the snarling shape. There was an extra-loud roar. "Got him!" he shouted. But the then ant-lion charged towards him, roaring more angrily than ever. The gang stood at the entrance with the cave ants, throwing stones in the dark. Gradually the roars and snarls grew less, then they stopped altogether.

"It's gone," said Emmet. "And with a sore head, most likely."

As dawn began to break, the gang went outside with Emmet and the cave ants. The ground was strewn with stones and marked with ant-lion footprints. The stones were all carefully brought back inside the cave and stacked in neat piles ready for the next time

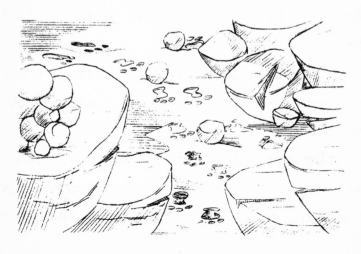

they would be needed.

"Does this happen often?" asked Alexi with a yawn, as they sat down to a cold breakfast.

"Only at full moon," said Emmet. "That's when the cave ant-lion and the cave woolly bear go hunting ants."

"But you don't stand guard in the daytime," said Ruby.

"No need," said Emmet. "Ant-lions and bears only do their hunting at night. Other things like sabre-toothed cen-tipedes and the giant wasp keep clear of the caves by day."

After breakfast everyone carried their fur rugs outside, and spread them on the rocks to air.

The gang sat outside in the sun with a crowd of cave ants around them. Alexi was explaining what it was like to have furniture and electricity, but they didn't understand.

"Perhaps you can explain a great mystery to us," said Emmet. "Come with us and we will show you."

"O.K.," said Anthony, and the gang set off with Emmet, his father and a dozen cave ants carrying thorn spears. "Just in case we meet something dangerous," said the Cave Leader.

"Or hungry," said Emmet.

The journey took them across a stretch of open ground. They hurried, keeping an eye open for giant wasps. Billy gripped his mirror in his pocket . . . just in case.

After a time they reached a rocky slope. Part way up was the entrance to a cave.

"It's empty nowadays," said Emmet. "But some very special ants must have lived here once. The cave is very deep.

The sun shines a long way in, but after that there seems to be no end to it, just darkness stretching on and on."

"Have we come all this way to see a deep, dark cave?" said Ruby in a whisper.

Emmet beckoned them forward. They entered the cave . . . and stopped in wonder. The rocky walls were covered

with pictures! Brightly coloured cave ant-lions, cave woolly bears, woolly rhinoceros beetles, and what could only be a giant elk beetle, reaching from floor to roof.

For once, Kevin couldn't think of anything to say.

"Now," said Emmet, "this is the real mystery. The ants who drew all these pictures were not only very clever artists, but something else besides. Because we

think that they could see in the dark!"

"What do you mean?" said Anthony.

"No matter how far you go into the cave," Emmet went on, "you will find pictures painted on the walls. We know because we sometimes find pieces of rock fallen down deep in the darkness. And when we take them outside, we see that they are painted too."

All the way back to the cave Anthony's mind was in a whirl. The world of the cave ants was weird, to say the very least. They ate lunch, cold of course, and tried not to notice that the fur they sat on was still damp. Suddenly, Anthony leapt to his feet.

"I've got it," he shouted. "Yes! Why did none of us think of it before? Emmet's speaking of people who could see in the dark. Of course! Give me your spectacles, Alexi!"

Alexi handed them over.

"Now," said Anthony excitedly, "I'm going to need lots of sticks. Can everyone help collect them for me, please?"

The Cave Leader nodded to his family, and all the cave ants scurried about bringing twigs and scraps of wood. They gathered around Anthony as he laid a piece of dry moss on the ground. Then, looking up at the sky, he held Alexi's

spectacles so that the rays of the sun made a bright spot on the moss.

The cave ants wondered what this strange young ant was up to.

A trickle of smoke appeared. The cave ants leaned forward to look.

A small flame flickered brightly, and they shrank back. Anthony fed small pieces of stick to the flame. In just a few minutes he had a crackling fire. The first ever fire seen by the cave ants.

"What is it?" asked the cave ants in wonder.

"Fire," said Anthony. "It can make you warm. It can cook your food. It gives off light so you can see. And . . . wild creatures are afraid of it."

"It's getting smaller," cried Emmet in alarm.

"Give it more wood," said Anthony. "You must feed it and look after it. If it dies you won't be able to light it again, so you must always have one fire alight. Then you can light others from it."

That night the cave was lit by a large fire burning in the centre of the floor. It made things a bit smoky, but the cave ants didn't seem to mind. They still sat down to a cold supper, but, as Ruby remarked, home cooking was something that had to be learned. And that would take time.

Before bedtime, Terry helped to pile up a huge heap of twigs in the cave entrance, and set it alight with a flaming stick from the fire in the centre of the cave. "Let a cave ant-lion try to get past that," said Anthony.

For the first time everyone in the cave slept peacefully through the night. Even the fur rugs didn't seem quite as damp as they were before.

In the morning, Anthony said, "We'll have to go back to our own land today, but before we go we'd like to see the painted cave again. Will you take us?"

Emmet and the Cave Leader led the way, and the gang followed. Ruby carried a clay pot very carefully as if it held something very precious. The rest of the gang carried long sticks with wads of dry moss tied around one end.

When they reached the cave, Ruby placed the pot on the ground and blew gently until a wisp of smoke appeared over the rim. More blowing and the smoke became a flame. In a moment she had lit the moss tied to the sticks. "Those," said Anthony, "are torches. The people who drew the pictures in the cave couldn't see in the dark. They used fire to make light."

Carrying the torches, the gang led the cave ants deep into the cave. There were pictures everywhere. In the flickering torchlight some of the painted creatures seemed to move.

"This is scary," said Billy, sticking close to Anthony.

As the torches began to burn low, they made their way back to the daylight.

Ruby put what was left of the glowing moss from the torches into the clay pot, and handed it to the old Cave Leader.

"You must always keep this alight," she said. "Even if all the fires in the cave die, this will rekindle them."

Soon it was time for the gang to go. The cave ants came part of the way, stopping when they came to a tall rock.

"This is the end of our country," said Emmet. "From here you must travel by yourselves."

"Before you go," said Emmet's father, "I want to thank you for the wonderful gift you have brought my people. We should like you to have these to remember us by." And to each of the gang he gave a flat grey stone with a pattern scratched on it, exactly like the one Anthony had found in his father's study.

"I would like to give you a gift too," Billy piped up. He took out his fragment of Bigfoot mirror and handed it to the Cave Leader. The old man took it. He shook Billy by the hand and said, "Thank you, Billy. We will always treasure it."

"Goodbye!" called the gang as they set off homewards.

They had left the Wildlands far behind

them when Ruby said, "Hush! Isn't that music I can hear?"

It was. The grasshopper was sitting on his pad of moss, fiddling merrily.

"I got some fiddle strings!" he cried. "Wrote a new tune. Call it 'Ants Went a-Travelling'. Want to hear it?"

It was a very catchy tune. Long after they had gone on their way, they could still hear the grasshopper playing. Kevin started to whistle. The others joined in.

"It needs words," said Ruby. She sang: "Ants went a-travelling, one by one. Off to the Wildlands, just for fun."

Kevin took up the tune: "Ants went a-travelling, two by two. Seemed like the coolest thing to do."

Then Billy: "Ants went a-travelling, three by three. Ne-ant-erthals they were hoping to see."

Then Terry added: "Ants went a-travelling, four by four. To hear the ant-lion rage and roar."

Alexi said, "I'm not a very good singer, but here goes: "Ants went a-travelling, five by five. Glad that they all came home alive."

And, finally, Anthony: "Ants went a-travelling, Anthony's gang. And as they travelled they laughed and sang."

And laugh and sing they did, all the rest of the way home to Antville.